11/95

D0819949

Orchard Books   New York

Mama Moon

Jeannine Ouellette Howitz • illustrated by Catherine Stock

Text copyright © 1995 by Jeannine Ouellette-Howitz. Illustrations copyright © 1995 by
Catherine Stock. All rights reserved. No part of this book may be reproduced or transmitted in
any form or by any means, electronic or mechanical, including photocopying, recording, or by
any information storage or retrieval system, without permission in writing from the Publisher.
Orchard Books, 95 Madison Avenue, New York, NY 10016. Manufactured in the United
States of America. Printed by Barton Press, Inc. Bound by Horowitz/Rae. Book design by
Catherine Stock. Calligraphy by Jean Krulis. The text of this book is set in 22 point Berkeley
Old Style Bold Italic. The illustrations are chalk pastel reproduced in full color.

Library of Congress Cataloging-in-Publication Data. Ouellette-Howitz, Jeannine. Mama moon
/ by Jeannine Ouellette-Howitz ; illustrated by Catherine Stock. p. cm. Summary: A little
girl is reassured as her mother explains about the baby growing inside her "magic room."
ISBN 0-531-09472-3. — ISBN 0-531-08772-7 (lib. bdg.) [1. Babies—Fiction.
2. Pregnancy—Fiction. 3. Mothers and daughters—Fiction.] I. Stock, Catherine, ill.
II. Title. PZ7.O895Mam 1995 [E]—dc20 95-732

In memory of
Nana and Lala,
with love
—J.O.H.

nce upon a wintertime,
a little girl named Sophie lay
tucked warmly into bed. She was
thinking of Mama's surprise.
Soon a baby would come, from
somewhere near and far . . .
Mama's room.

It was too quiet to sleep, so Sophie took her favorite blanket, soft and frayed just right at the silky edges. She padded downstairs and found Mama rocking by the window, where the moon pressed its fullness against the night.
"Mama, will you hold me for a little minute?"

Sophie curled around Mama's great round belly and remembered what Mama had said, about all women having rooms, even little girls, even Sophie. She put her hand low on her own belly, on the soft, warm spot where her room was supposed to be.

She held her breath. Nothing.

Then Sophie closed her eyes, and she found herself suddenly alone in a magic room. It was bare, except for a ceiling of twinkling stars and a wooden cradle with a butterfly carved into the headboard. The cradle was made up with a flannel quilt, brand-new and just right for baby.

But when Sophie lifted the quilt,
the cradle was empty.

Sophie's eyes flew open, and she
sat up straight. "Mama, how do
you know for sure there's a baby
in your magic room?"

Mama laughed. "It's a womb,
not a room. And I'll show you
how I know." Mama placed Sophie's
little hand over her big belly, and
the swollen womb beneath it.
It was hard and still, but then
Sophie felt a little kick, and a
jump and flutter as the baby
danced inside.

"There is a baby!" Sophie sighed. She longed to jump and dance like the baby, but she was too tired, so she curled up and pressed both hands against her own hollow belly once more.

When Sophie closed her eyes,
she was back in the magic room.
It wasn't empty anymore. Dad,
Grandma, Grandpa, aunts, and
uncles were all gathered around
Mama, who was wrapped
in a bright robe with golden
butterflies stitched around
the collar. Mama
was smiling and
holding a tiny baby.

When Sophie said,
"Excuse me!" and tried to scoot through the
others to Mama, no one noticed or heard.

Sophie opened her eyes, and a tear squeezed out and rolled down her cheek. She pressed her wet face into Mama's neck. "Oh, Mama, who will hold me after the baby comes?"

"I will, honey," answered Mama, hugging Sophie tighter. "Grandma says that with each baby a mother's arms grow stronger and her heart bigger. As long as I'm your mama, there will be room for you in my heart and in my arms . . . and right here on my lap."

Sophie felt warm and sleepy, and her heavy eyes fell shut. One more time, she touched the special place over her magic womb, right where she had felt the baby move in Mama.

Very slowly then, something inside of Sophie began to flutter and unfold, until the whole room was a vision of stained glass butterflies dancing brightly in the air. They tickled Sophie's cheeks with their gold-red-purple-green wings, and gave her soft butterfly kisses to make her laugh.

Mama held Sophie close
and hummed lullabies of butterfly
wings and magic moons . . .
and a brand-new baby coming soon
as they rocked back and forth.

After a little minute, Mama carried Sophie upstairs, tucked her back into bed, and kissed her first sleeping baby good-night.